BERTA
A REMARKABLE DOG

BERTA
A REMARKABLE DOG

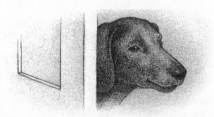

CELIA BARKER LOTTRIDGE

WITH PICTURES BY
Elsa Myotte

A GROUNDWOOD BOOK
DOUGLAS & McINTYRE
TORONTO VANCOUVER BUFFALO

Groundwood Books/Douglas & McIntyre
720 Bathurst Street, Suite 500, Toronto, Ontario M5S 2R4

Distributed in the USA by Publishers Group West
1700 Fourth Street, Berkeley, CA 94710

We acknowledge the support of the Canada Council for the Arts, the
Ontario Arts Council and the Government of Canada through the Book
Publishing Industry Development Program for our publishing activities.

ONTARIO ARTS COUNCIL
CONSEIL DES ARTS DE L'ONTARIO

National Library of Canada Cataloguing in Publication Data
Lottridge, Celia B. (Celia Barker)
Berta : a remarkable dog
ISBN 0-88899-461-3 (bound). ISBN 0-88899-469-9 (pbk.)
I. Myotte, Elsa   II. Title.
PS8573.O855B47 2002   jC813'.54   C2001-903209-9
PZ7.L918Be 2002

Design by Michael Solomon
Printed and bound in Canada

To Lucy and Jonathan
and the dogs we have known

Table of Contents

CHAPTER 1
A REMARKABLE DOG

Berta lived in the small town of Middle Westfield in a yellow house with a barn behind it. She was a dog. A very remarkable dog. Most people who knew her thought she was quite ordinary, but they were wrong. The day would come when Berta would do something surprising. Something remarkable.

Berta was a sturdy dog with smooth brown fur. She had a long pointed nose and floppy ears. She also had very short legs.

"She looks like a sausage," said Rosalind

Mahoney who lived next door to the yellow house. "She's a sausage dog."

"No, she isn't," said Marjory Miller. Marjory was part of Berta's family. She was nine years old and Rosalind was her best friend. "I have told you at least fifty times. Berta is a dachshund. Dachshunds are supposed to have short legs. They were bred to hunt badgers. They can dig very fast and corner the badgers underground, in holes. If they had long legs they could never do that."

The dog they were discussing was curled in a doughnut shape on Marjory's bed. Her eyes were closed.

Rosalind looked at her.

"Berta would never be bothered to dig holes and go into them for any reason," she said. "She's too lazy. If any badgers lived in Middle Westfield they wouldn't have to worry."

Marjory had to agree that Berta was not a very energetic dog. Her favorite pastimes were eating and sleeping and, if necessary, taking short walks. Certainly not hunting. Other animals didn't interest her at all. If a neighborhood kitten pounced on her tail while she was resting under the lilac bush Berta just closed her eyes. And she never bothered to go down to the little barn where Mr. Miller kept chickens and pigs and the occasional calf.

"Maybe Berta doesn't want to hunt," Marjory said, "but when she does want something she is very determined. For instance, she knows perfectly well that she is not supposed to be on my bed, but if you tried to move her right now she would make herself as heavy as a big stone."

Berta opened her eyes halfway and gave Rosalind a long look.

"Don't worry, Berta," Rosalind said

quickly. "I wouldn't dream of moving you."

Berta closed her eyes and Marjory smiled. This was a dog who always knew exactly what she wanted and she almost always got it without making a fuss. Marjory was the only person who noticed. Even her parents, who had known Berta since puppyhood, only said things like, "Thank goodness Berta is such a quiet dog. No trouble at all."

When Rosalind had gone home Marjory gave Berta a hug and a pat.

"Someday you'll show people how clever you are, won't you?" she said.

And Berta did. She was, after all, a very remarkable dog.

CHAPTER 2
A BOX OF CHICKS

It was March, a bothersome month in Middle Westfield. Not winter and not spring. Marjory was tired of wearing her fat winter jacket, but if she changed to a thinner one she got cold to the bone playing outside at recess.

Marjory's mother, who taught biology at the high school, said, "I know that Nature needs this wretched month for some reason, but why does it have to last such a long time?"

Even Berta seemed restless. She whined

at the door, took one look at the patchy snow in the yard and refused to go out. A few minutes later she was whining at the door again.

Only Mr. Miller enjoyed March. He ran the hardware store in Middle Westfield but even more than hardware, he loved farm animals. That is why he wanted to live in a very small town.

"In Middle Westfield I can have farm animals without the bother of a farm," he liked to say, and it was true. No one in town minded a flock of chickens, some ducks, a few pigs and maybe a calf or two. So the Millers lived in a house with a barn where Mr. Miller could keep his animals. In March he always looked forward to the arrival of some new ones in time for spring.

"I've ordered fifty baby chicks from the hatchery," he told Marjory one Saturday morning. "They'll arrive at the post office today. Do you want to come with me to get them?"

"Oh, yes," said Marjory. Every year it amazed her that boxes of chicks came to the post office just like any other packages. Of course, the boxes had holes punched all around the sides so that the chicks could breathe, and they were shallow so that the chicks would not pile up on top of each other. And they came express post so that the chicks would get to their new homes as soon as possible.

When Marjory and her dad walked into the post office they knew immediately that the chicks were there. They could hear them cheeping. The cheeping was surprisingly loud because many boxes of chicks had come in that day for all the people around Middle Westfield who raised chickens. There were big boxes with one hundred chicks and smaller ones with fifty.

The postmistress handed Mr. Miller one of the smaller boxes.

"You'll have to keep these fellows indoors for a while," she said. "Too cold for them outside right now."

"We've got a nice warm spot all ready," said Mr. Miller. He put the box in the back seat of the car and he and Marjory drove home.

The place reserved for the chicks was in the storeroom off the kitchen. As soon as her dad set the box on the floor Marjory lifted off the lid. There were fifty fuzzy yellow chicks huddled in the corners of the box.

"You must hate being shut up and moved around in the dark," Marjory said to them. "Don't worry, you're home now."

"They only hatched the day before yesterday," said Mr. Miller, "so they don't know what to expect. But I bet they'd like some food and water." He put chick mash in two bowls and water in two more and set them down in the box. Then he put a desk lamp beside the box, close enough for the bulb to keep the chicks warm.

"In a week or so they'll have some feathers and be big enough to move to the barn," he said. "This will keep them happy for now."

Marjory sat watching the chicks begin to walk around. Some found the mash and began pecking at it. She hoped they were happy. She picked one chick up and felt its little poky feet prickling the palm of her hand. When she put it down it cuddled into a corner with most of the others and went to sleep.

That's about all chicks did, she remembered. When they were cute they cheeped and slept. Then they turned into chickens. Marjory was not very fond of chickens.

She said good-bye to the chicks and went over to Rosalind's house.

At suppertime Mr. Miller looked in on the chicks before he sat down at the kitchen table.

"They're doing fine," he said. "I can almost believe they're bigger now than they were when we brought them home."

Berta was curled up beside the radiator in the corner. She always spent mealtimes in that spot pretending to be asleep. Marjory knew that she really was watching through her eyelashes, ready to get up quietly if a crust of bread or a strand of spaghetti landed on the floor. Berta did not let any food go to waste.

Tonight she saw Berta open her eyes and look at the family eating and talking. Then she got up but she didn't come to the table. Instead she walked stealthily, with her toenails clicking just a little on the tile, to the storeroom door. It was open a crack and Berta gently pushed at it with her nose until it opened just a little more. Then she disappeared through the opening.

Marjory stopped eating lasagna. Why would Berta want to go into the storeroom? Maybe she had heard the chicks and was investigating the sound. Well, thought Marjory, I had better investigate Berta.

She got up from the table and pushed the door wide open. There was the box of chicks with the light shining down on them. And there was Berta with her nose in among the chicks.

"What are you doing, Berta?" said Marjory. "Are you sniffing them? They're just baby chickens."

She looked more closely. Berta had her mouth open. Marjory could see her long pink tongue. Was she eating the chicks?

For a moment Marjory couldn't move

or make a sound. Then she saw that long pink tongue skimming over the heads of the chicks.

Berta was licking the chicks. She was doing her best to wash them, following them around the box with her nose and lapping at them with her tongue.

The chicks did not want to be washed. They were scrambling away from the large damp thing that had suddenly appeared above them but Berta would not give up.

Marjory found her voice.

"Berta, stop!" she said and grabbed her dog by the collar. She pulled her out of the storeroom and shut the door firmly. Berta gave her a resentful look and went back to the radiator where she curled up with her back to the room.

"What was all that about? Was Berta doing something to the chicks?" said Mrs. Miller.

"She was licking them," said Marjory. "She didn't hurt them. They just got a little wet. But why would she want to lick those fuzzy things? She never did before."

"I don't know," said Mrs. Miller, "but we'd better keep the storeroom door shut tight. Berta might drown a chick with that big tongue of hers."

But Berta didn't even look at the storeroom door after that, as far as Marjory could tell.

"Probably she was just curious," she said to herself. But she wondered.

CHAPTER 3
BEWARE THE PIG

The chicks were still living in the storeroom when Mr. Miller burst through the
back door early the next Saturday morning
with a wide grin on his face.

"Great news," he said to his sleepy family. "We have six new baby pigs. Born last
night. Prettiest piglets you ever saw."

Marjory smiled back at her dad. He
thought pigs were the best of all animals.
She liked them quite well, too, but she
would never call them pretty. Still, baby
pigs could certainly be called cute. She

decided to visit them right after breakfast.

March was still being miserable so she
put on her warm jacket even though the
barn was only a two-minute walk away.

"Wear your old boots," said her mother.
"It's so muddy around the barn."

Marjory picked her way across the
muddy yard, shivering in the raw wind.
She was glad to get into the shelter of the
barn and pull the big door shut behind her.
She loved the barn. It had three stalls
downstairs and a loft above. Rosalind liked
to say it was really an overgrown shed, but
it felt like a barn and it smelled of clean and
well-fed animals. The air was strangely
warm.

Dad said that was because of the pigs.

"They used to build animal sheds right
next to the farm houses just for the
warmth," he told her.

Marjory liked to imagine a house with a pig standing patiently in each room in place of a radiator, giving off heat.

It would be smelly but interesting, she decided. But the pigs would probably get bored.

Right now two of the stalls were empty and one was full of the mother pig and her six piglets. Marjory leaned on the railing and smiled at the sight of them. She had forgotten how big the mother pig was and how small the piglets would look next to her. They were Hampshire pigs, which meant they were black with neat belts of white around their middles. The mother pig lay on her side like a mountain with all the babies neatly lined up along her belly, nursing.

It was very quiet. Marjory could hear the piglets snuffle a little as they sucked, but the mother seemed to be asleep.

Then she heard another sound, like very quiet footsteps.

There was cold air blowing into the barn. The door had come open. And something was pushing against Marjory's ankles.

She looked down.

"Berta," she said. "What are you doing? You never come into the barn."

Berta paid no attention. She was beside Marjory, sticking her nose between the slats of the stall railing. She seemed to be trying to push herself right into the stall.

The mother pig lifted her head. Her little shiny eyes looked straight at Berta. Her ears twitched and a sound like the creaking of a rusty hinge came from her throat.

Marjory grabbed Berta's collar and pulled hard.

"Berta, you can't go in there. That pig is getting mad," she said sharply.

She pulled until even the tip of Berta's

nose was safely outside the railing. Then she took a quick look into the pen, without letting go of the collar.

The mother pig had laid her head back down, but her eyes were open and watchful. The piglets were still lying peacefully in their row, sucking.

"Come on, Berta," said Marjory firmly. "You don't belong in the barn. Remember, you're a house dog."

Berta trotted ahead of her out the open door. "You're getting too good at opening doors," Marjory said and led the way back to the house.

At dinner that night she told her parents all about it. Her dad shook his head.

"Pigs are fierce mothers," he said. "Berta had better stay away from the barn."

"I know," said Marjory. She imagined Berta squashed flat under a huge mother pig. "I'll keep my eye on her."

"I wonder what has gotten into our quiet dog?" said Mrs. Miller. "She's always liked comfort above everything. Why is she interested in the pigs all of a sudden? It's just not like her."

Marjory remembered the chicks. That was strange, too. She looked at Berta who was curled up in her usual spot. She wasn't even pretending to be asleep. She was watching Marjory. Then she winked.

"But dogs don't wink," Marjory told herself.

She wondered what would happen next.

Marjory was walking slowly home from school. Rosalind had a dentist appointment so she was all alone. It was a nice day for a walk. The sky was blue and the air was almost warm. It was easy to think that spring was near, but Marjory knew that it really wouldn't come until sometime in April, and April was still weeks away.

She was just crossing the street in front of her house when she saw Berta running across the yard.

Marjory stopped and stared. Berta never

ran unless someone was holding something very delicious and calling her. But there was no one in sight.

And where was Berta going? She wasn't heading for the back door, and she was paying no attention to Marjory. She was running around to the front of the house with her head down, as if she was hiding something.

Sneaky, thought Marjory. That's how she looks. Sneaky.

Marjory began to run, too. She cut across the yard hoping to catch Berta before she disappeared. She seemed to be heading for the space under the front porch where old flower pots were stored.

"Stop, Berta," she called, but she knew it was useless. Berta was not going to stop. She was determined to do something that was either very important to her or very bad. Or maybe both.

Marjory dropped her books and grabbed Berta around the middle with both hands just as she was about to disappear under the porch.

"What are you doing, you silly dog?" she said. She sat down on the bottom step and held Berta by the collar so that she could look her in the eye.

But Berta wouldn't look at her.

"It's okay. I won't get mad. What's the matter?" But Berta kept her chin down and her head twisted away.

"I know what it is," said Marjory, getting a little cross. "You have something you're not supposed to have. Maybe something really yucky. Well, I have to see it."

She put one hand under Berta's chin and Berta suddenly looked up.

There, sticking out of her mouth, was a tail. A little spiky tail with black fur.

"Oh, Berta," Marjory whispered. "You

can't have a whole animal in your mouth. You just can't." But she knew that Berta could. And did.

Berta blinked but she did not open her mouth.

Marjory drew a deep breath.

"Drop it, Berta," she said quietly but very firmly. "Drop it!" And even though she did not know what might fall out of Berta's mouth, she kept one hand under her chin.

Berta slowly opened her mouth and a tiny kitten fell out into Marjory's hand. It was curled up so that she couldn't see whether it was hurt, but its black fur was damp and it wasn't moving at all.

She let go of Berta's collar and held the kitten in both hands. Even though she was worried about what she might see, she looked the kitten over as well as she could without moving it around. It was so young that its eyes weren't open.

"Oh, please. Be alive," whispered Marjory. "Please be alive."

The kitten lay perfectly still for an endless moment. Then it opened its mouth very wide and gave a tiny squeaking *meew*.

"Thank goodness," said Marjory. She could breathe again. She looked at Berta who was staring at the kitten in her hands. "Why did you steal a kitten, Berta? And what were you going to do with it? I wish you could talk."

She got up, leaving her books lying on the ground. "Come on, Berta. We've got to tell Mom what you've brought home."

Her mother was sitting at the kitchen table marking papers but she got up and opened the door when she heard Marjory calling.

"What do you have there?" she asked. "Is something wrong?"

Marjory held out her cupped hands so

that her mother could see what she was carrying.

"A kitten," said Mrs. Miller. "Where on earth did you find such a tiny one? It should be with its mother."

"It wasn't me," said Marjory. "It was Berta. She kidnapped this kitten. She brought it home in her mouth and I saw its tail sticking out. Oh, Mom, I was so scared it would be dead."

Mrs. Miller took the kitten from her gently and looked it over carefully.

"It looks fine," she said, "but it does need to get back to its mother."

"Probably it belongs to one of Jenny Jefferson's cats. There are always kittens in her shed. I'll take it over there," said Marjory. "But, Mom, why would Berta steal a kitten? She's being so strange. Why would she want to get into the pig pen? And why would she lick the chicks?"

Mrs. Miller looked at Berta who was sitting beside her staring longingly up at the kitten.

"I guess it's babies," she said. "Berta has never had puppies and she probably feels it's time. I'm sorry, Berta. There are so many animals around this place in the spring that I don't want puppies, too. In the fall we can find a nice father for your pups. Wouldn't you like to have puppies in the fall?"

"Poor Berta," said Marjory. "How can she understand?"

She got a soft cloth to make a nest for the kitten and carried it over to Jenny Jefferson's house. Jenny was a tiny gray-haired woman who cared for cats above all else. She had five of her own, fed many more and always found good homes for the kittens that were born in her shed.

She looked at the black kitten and said, "Why that's one of Midnight's litter. You say your dog stole it? Must be a very gentle dog. The kitten is fine but you keep that dog away."

"We will," said Marjory. "She has never done such a thing before. Will Midnight take the kitten back?"

"I'm going to rub it all over with a towel the kittens have been sleeping on," said Jenny. "That should do the trick. Midnight is a good mother. She'll take it back."

Marjory walked home feeling sorry for Berta. She had carried that kitten home so gently, just because she wanted babies of her own.

I'll let her sleep on my bed tonight, she decided. And I'll tell her that next fall isn't so far away. If only she could understand.

CHAPTER 5
A KNOCK ON THE DOOR

$\mathcal{B}y$ *the next* $\mathcal{S}aturday$ every hint of spring was gone. The sky was gray and the wind whipped scraps of sleet against the windows.

"At least it's not a school day," said Rosalind. "I don't mind walking as far as your house on a day like this, but school? No thank you."

Marjory agreed. It was a day to stay home. She and Rosalind had spent the morning making chocolate chip cookies. Berta was upstairs, probably sleeping on

Marjory's bed. She knew from experience that nobody ever gave her treats when they were baking, so she didn't bother to hang about hoping for handouts.

Now all the cookies were baked and the girls were cleaning up the flour that had somehow spread itself evenly over every flat surface in the kitchen. Marjory stopped to admire the rows of enticing brown cookies cooling on the racks. Not even one was burned and they had taken care of the few broken ones by eating them.

Her mother came into the kitchen and said, "Those are gorgeous cookies and the smell is driving me crazy but let's don't eat any till after lunch. I have some chili in the fridge. You girls can peel carrots for carrot sticks. And of course dessert is just waiting there, thanks to you."

In two minutes the table was set and the chili was warming on the stove.

Just then there was a knock at the back door.

"Would you see who that is, Rosalind?" said Mrs. Miller, who was stirring the chili. "I'm not expecting anyone but there's plenty of food."

Rosalind opened the door and a man stepped into the kitchen. The wind banged the storm door behind him and he stood wiping his boots on the mat.

"This is some terrible day," he said. He was wearing a hat with earflaps and a plaid wool jacket. Marjory thought that he was carrying something inside the jacket, holding it against his chest as if it needed protecting.

"Why, it's Jack Steiner, isn't it," said Mrs. Miller. "I didn't recognize you at first in that hat. What brings you to town?"

"Well, I wouldn't have come if I didn't have a problem," said Mr. Steiner. "You know I raise sheep and it's lambing time. Not a good time to be away but my wife said she could look after things for a couple of hours and I have this little fellow to worry about."

"What little fellow?' said Marjory.

"He's right here," said Mr. Steiner, patting the left side of his jacket. "I had to keep him out of the wind. He was just born this morning, you know."

Marjory started to speak but her mother said, "Tell us about him."

"I have this ewe," said Mr. Steiner. "She's a good mother but cranky and she had twins this time, both fine healthy lambs. But she only wants to take care of one of them. She'll have nothing to do with this one, though he's big and healthy."

He stopped talking and looked around the kitchen. "I guess your husband isn't home?"

"No, he's down at the store," said Mrs. Miller. Suddenly she smiled. "Now I understand. You have a lamb that needs a home and Tom always likes to give a home to a baby farm animal."

"Well, yes," said Mr. Steiner. "I thought you folks might like to have a lamb to raise. He has to be fed with a bottle and I just don't have the time and I know Tom Miller would take good care of him."

"Please, could we see him?" said Marjory. She didn't know whether her mom would want a lamb, but surely if she saw him she couldn't resist.

Jack Steiner unbuttoned his jacket and took out a bundle wrapped in a green towel. He set it on a chair and carefully folded back the cloth.

Marjory and Rosalind came close and saw a small heap of grayish white wool and a little face with a black nose and black eyes blinking in the light of the kitchen.

"Easy, little guy," said Mr. Steiner.

"Can I hold him?" asked Marjory.

"Sure you can. Sit down and I'll put him in your lap."

The lamb felt solid and warm even through the towel. Marjory and Rosalind gently touched his wool, and he shivered his skin as if he liked being touched.

Mrs. Miller watched for a moment and then said, "I'd say the decision is made as long as you girls promise to help with the feeding. I have a feeling that lambs like to eat often."

"You're right about that," said Jack Steiner. "Every two hours the first week, I'm afraid. Then every four hours for a week. Aside from that, lambs are pretty sturdy. Just keep him warm till he's put on a little weight."

"But what do we feed him?" asked Mrs. Miller.

"Glad you asked," said the farmer. "I almost forgot. I brought you some ewe's milk to start him out on. When that's gone just give him regular cow's milk. And I brought you some special nipples to feed him with. Just put one on a pop bottle. I'll get them from the truck and then I'd better get back. There will be some new lambs to look after when I get home, I expect. Oh, by the way, I raise these lambs for wool. If you don't want to shear him just bring him back to me."

When he was gone Mrs. Miller said, "It's a good thing for this lamb that I said yes before I heard about feeding him every two hours." Rosalind laughed but Marjory hardly heard. She was looking at the small animal lying in her lap.

"A lamb," she said. "When I woke up

this morning I didn't know we would have a lamb by lunchtime."

"Speaking of lunch, I'd better find a box to put your new friend in. I don't think you can eat and hold a lamb in your lap at the same time."

Mrs. Miller hurried off and came back with a square cardboard box with an old blanket in it. She set it in the warmest corner of the room, the one where Berta always napped. Then she picked up the lamb and put him in the box. He lay there looking suddenly very small and lonely.

"We should give him a name," said Marjory. "Maybe he'll feel more at home when we know what to call him. But what's a good name for a lamb?"

"I know the perfect name," said Rosalind. "Today is the seventeenth of March. St. Patrick's Day. Notice my green socks. Anyway, I think you should name him Patrick since St. Patrick's Day is his birthday."

"Patrick," said Marjory, trying it out. "Patrick. I think it's a good name."

"So do I," said her mother.

But Patrick the lamb still looked small and lonely.

I can't hold him on my lap all the time, thought Marjory. But what else can I do to make him feel at home?

Then the door opened. Not the back door but the door into the living room. It was shut to keep the kitchen warm and cozy. Now it creaked open and Berta walked in.

Everyone stared at her, all thinking the same thing.

What would Berta think of Patrick? What would she do?

Berta looked at Marjory, who usually

greeted her with a pat, but Marjory didn't move or speak. Then she looked around the room and saw the box. She stood still looking at this strange object sitting in her special warm spot. Then, without hurrying, she walked right over to see exactly what it was.

She looked over the edge of the box, stretching her neck just a little.

There was Patrick the lamb looking back at her.

For a moment Berta and Patrick just looked at each other.

Then Berta jumped. With one smooth motion she was over the side of the box and standing beside Patrick. She sniffed him carefully from head to tail and seemed satisfied. Then she lay down and curled herself around him. When she was nicely settled she raised her head and looked at Mrs. Miller and Marjory and Rosalind.

"She isn't going to move," said Marjory.

"She looks totally determined," said Rosalind.

"I know what it is," said Mrs. Miller. "Berta has found herself a baby."

The instant Marjory heard her mother say, "Berta has found herself a baby," she knew that it was true. Berta was exactly where she wanted to be, curled protectively around Patrick, who was looking much larger as Berta's baby than he had as a lonely lamb. Berta lay perfectly still, but her eyes were alert, watching the three people standing around her.

"Berta is a dog," said Rosalind. "How can she be a mother to a lamb? Anyway, she's too small. Patrick is a baby but he's already taller than Berta. You'll see as soon as he stands up."

"That doesn't matter," said Marjory. "Berta is determined and she knows Patrick needs her. She'll figure out what to do."

"And we'll help her," said Mrs. Miller. "We'll have to do the feeding, for one thing. No matter how determined she is, Berta can't produce milk for a lamb."

Just then Berta lifted her head and gave a sort of whining yelp. When nothing happened she yelped again.

Marjory said, "What do you want, Berta?"

Berta uncurled herself and sat up on her haunches. She looked at Patrick who was moving restlessly beside her. Then she yelped louder.

Mrs. Miller looked at her watch.

"Oh," she said. "It must be time to feed this lamb. I suppose it's been about two hours since he left the farm. Are you hungry, Patrick?"

She went to the refrigerator and got out the bottle of milk Jack Steiner had left.

"How did Berta know?" asked Rosalind.

"Maybe she could feel him getting restless, or maybe she could hear his stomach growling," said Mrs. Miller.

"Maybe she just knows these things now that she's his mother," said Marjory.

"Don't go thinking mothers know everything," said Mrs. Miller. "But right now I know that Patrick isn't the only one who needs feeding. You serve up the chili, Marjory, and I'll get Patrick started."

She warmed some of the milk, poured it into a big pop bottle and snapped on the extra long nipple. When she held it out to Patrick, he began to suck on it greedily. Berta lay down, but she didn't take her eyes off Patrick and the bottle.

They spent lunchtime taking turns holding the bottle and eating their chili. By the time they got to the cookies, Patrick and Berta were both asleep, curled up together.

All afternoon Marjory resisted the temptation to call her father and tell him about Patrick. It was hard, but she decided that it was too good a surprise to ruin. At six o'clock she volunteered to set the table so that she would be on hand when he came in the door.

"Tom never gets home till twenty past. How long can you spend setting the table?" teased her mother.

Marjory didn't answer, but she had never set the table so carefully. She folded the napkins into triangles and lined up the knives, forks and spoons perfectly. She even found some green candles in the back of a cupboard and made a St. Patrick's Day centerpiece.

She was just thinking about drawing a picture to decorate each place when the back door opened.

"What's this? A party? Is it somebody's birthday?" said her father.

"Actually it is," said Marjory. "Somebody you've never met, but he's come to live with us. Look." She led him over to the box.

Mr. Miller looked down at Patrick.

"A lamb? What is a lamb doing in our kitchen?" he said. "I'm sure he wasn't here when I left home this morning. And what is Berta doing in there with him? Did she find a lamb to bring home this time?"

While he took off his coat and boots Marjory told him the whole story.

"And Berta has adopted him. She's decided to be his mother," she finished up.

"I don't suppose Berta will take on all

the responsibility," said her father. "What do we know about feeding this baby?"

"He has to eat every two hours for the first week. But I'll help. I'll take my turn."

"Not in the night," said her mother. "You need your sleep. Anyway, Tom and I have had experience getting up to feed a baby. We'll do the night shift."

And her father said the same thing when it was bedtime.

"You have to understand that I've always wanted to raise a lamb. I look forward to getting up at midnight and two o'clock and four o'clock and six."

"I'll get up at two," said her mother. "That's not so bad."

"I can do the six o'clock one," said Marjory. "I almost get up at six anyway."

"Six in the morning is quite different than seven," said her father. "But set your alarm. I'll be glad not to get up at six."

So Marjory set her alarm and fell asleep reminding herself that it was her responsibility to actually wake up when it went off. There was a baby to be fed.

She dreamed about sheep all night, and about Berta who had grown large and was herding many sheep into the barn. One little one kept wandering off and Berta ran after it, barking. The barking got louder and louder until Marjory opened her eyes.

The room was very dark and the barking didn't stop. It wasn't part of her dream any more. She fumbled for her lamp switch. When the light came on, the room was suddenly quiet. Marjory, squinting in the brightness, saw Berta beside the bed, staring at her and then looking at the door.

Suddenly Marjory remembered. Patrick. She was supposed to feed Patrick. Her clock said 6:15.

"Oh, Berta, I'm sorry. I didn't hear my

alarm. But I guess you did and then you had to wake me up."

Berta was not listening. She was going to the top of the stairs and coming back. It was clear that she wanted Marjory to hurry up. So Marjory hurried. She put on her slippers and bathrobe and went slowly down the stairs. She didn't feel very awake and she didn't want to stumble.

Patrick was waiting. He struggled to his feet when he heard them coming and looked over the side of the box. Marjory wanted to pick him up and hug him, but she didn't. She got out the bottle she and her mother had fixed the night before. She set it in a pan of warm water to take the chill off and then she offered it to Patrick.

He opened his mouth and closed it around the nipple and began to suck so hard that Marjory almost dropped the bottle. She sat down and got a better grip.

Berta lay next to her and watched Patrick eat.

When her parents came down an hour later they found Patrick and Berta curled up together in the box and Marjory lying sound asleep on the rug with the empty bottle in her hand.

She woke up when she smelled bacon and toast.

"It's hard to get up early when you're not used to it," she said at breakfast.

"I noticed that you needed two wake-up alarms," said her father. When she looked puzzled he went on. "First I heard your alarm clock ring for a long time and then I heard barking. I was sure the barking wouldn't stop until you woke up, so I just put my head under the pillow and went back to sleep."

"I didn't hear my alarm clock," said Marjory. "But I guess Berta did and she knew I was supposed to feed Patrick so she made sure I woke up."

"Remarkable for Berta to figure that out," said Mrs. Miller. "Very surprising."

Marjory just smiled and went on eating toast and jam. She was still sleepy but she wasn't surprised. Not at all.

Taking care of Patrick was a big job for Berta. Marjory could see that. Having decided that Patrick was her baby, Berta settled down to look after him completely. She slept in the box with him, watched him anxiously when he took a few wobbly steps around the kitchen and breathed a sigh of relief when he was safely curled up beside her.

When she felt it was time for him to be fed she sat up in the box and gave one sharp yip. If no one came immediately with a bottle she got out of the box and stood by the refrigerator, barking occasionally until someone said, "Oh, yes, Berta. I know, it's time to feed the baby," and went and got the milk. Then she watched every move the person holding the bottle made. Marjory could imagine her saying, "You're holding the bottle too high." Or she might say to Patrick, "Don't be so greedy. There's plenty of milk."

Marjory loved to feed Patrick because he ate with so much enthusiasm. He stretched out his neck and braced his feet and sucked so hard she expected all the milk to disappear inside him in one long gulp. When he was finished he lay down looking completely satisfied and fell asleep immediately. Berta curled up beside him looking satisfied, too.

"You're a good mother, Berta," Marjory said to her. "Patrick is a lucky

lamb. You are the best mother he could have."

There was one problem. Berta, being a dog, felt that she should keep her baby clean by licking him. Patrick, being a lamb, was very hard to lick. He was not covered with nice smooth fur but with curly wool that was a bit oily. Dust stuck to it so that Patrick, though very cute, was pale gray instead of snowy white.

"I don't think ewes worry about keeping their lambs clean," said Mr. Miller. He and Marjory were watching Berta lick Patrick's back. She had to stand up to do it and she had been working from his shoulders back, licking and licking, for a long time. The part she had licked looked a little cleaner than the rest but there was a lot of Patrick still to wash. Marjory felt tired just watching her.

Finally Berta stopped. She lay down

beside Patrick and lay there with her eyes open and her tongue hanging out a little.

"She's thinking," said Marjory. "She's trying to decide how she can keep Patrick clean.

"I think it's a hopeless task," said her dad. "Lambs were not meant to be licked. You just have to let them get grubby. There's no other way."

The next day Marjory saw Berta licking Patrick again. She was lying beside him licking a spot on his shoulder that she could comfortably reach. After a while she stopped and Marjory went to see what she had accomplished.

There on Patrick's shoulder was a patch of fluffy white wool about the size of a playing card.

"Wow, Berta, you got him really clean in that spot," said Marjory. "When are you going to do the rest?"

But Berta never did. She had found a

way to keep a small part of Patrick as clean as she thought he should be. She was not going to try to do the impossible job of washing all of her large baby.

"I guess she thinks that we should do our part, too," Marjory told her dad. "We could try washing him."

"Well, I draw the line at washing a lamb," he answered. "I think Patrick looks very distinguished with that white mark on his shoulder. It shows that he is Berta's baby."

And that was the way it stayed. After three days Berta and Patrick had settled into a comfortable routine of eating and sleeping and a little bit of washing.

On the fourth day Marjory brought two friends home from school with her. One, of course, was Rosalind who had not seen Patrick since the day he arrived. The other was Russell Wilcox, a boy in their class who lived just down the street and had a scientific interest in animals. He had many pets including a white rat and a descented skunk, but he had never had a lamb. Naturally he wanted to meet Patrick.

The three of them came stomping and laughing into the kitchen and the door banged behind them.

Marjory was struggling with her jacket zipper when Russell said, "What's the matter with your dog?"

She looked up and saw Berta sitting up in the box with her teeth bared. Rosalind was still laughing so Marjory couldn't hear, but she was sure that Berta was growling. She opened her mouth to say, "We'd better quiet down. Berta is getting upset," but before she could speak Rosalind was kneeling beside the box.

"Oh, you adorable baby," she said and stuck out her hand to touch Patrick.

Berta opened her mouth and in a split second she had closed it on Rosalind's wrist. Marjory stared in horror waiting for Rosalind to yell or cry but she just sat without moving at all with her wrist between Berta's teeth. Russell was staring, too.

"She isn't actually biting you, is she?" he finally asked in a quiet voice.

"No," said Rosalind shakily. "She's just holding on. She won't let go."

Then Marjory could speak. "It's all right, Berta," she said. "Rosalind won't hurt Patrick. You can let go."

Berta turned her eyes around to look at Marjory and her forehead wrinkled up. She waited just a moment longer and then she opened her mouth a little.

Rosalind carefully slid her wrist out. Then she sat back on her heels and took a deep breath.

"Berta didn't like that, did she?" she said.

"I guess it's part of her job to protect Patrick," said Marjory.

"But she didn't think you were a serious threat," said Russell. "If she had she would have really bitten you."

"Thank goodness," said Rosalind. "But after all these years I should hope she would know I wouldn't hurt Patrick." She looked at Berta. "But I get the message. I'll never do it again. I promise."

After that they all sat quietly around the box and watched Patrick. They even patted him but they checked to make sure it was all right with Berta before they did.

Russell said, "Patrick is living a very unusual life for a lamb. He's in a house, not a barn. He's fed without having to scramble. And he has his own personal dog to protect him."

"And he has a mark on his shoulder to show how special he is," said Marjory, and she told them why Patrick had a white patch. "I guess it's all part of the job. Washing, protecting."

"And Patrick just thinks it's normal," said Rosalind. And they all laughed, but quietly.

CHAPTER 8
GROWING

Patrick grew. He grew very fast. He took up more and more space in his sleeping box and when he was on his feet he looked tall and wide, especially when he stood next to Berta.

None of this made any difference to Berta. She went right on curling up next to him in the box. She made sure he got fed and she licked the white spot on his shoulder every day.

Patrick didn't seem to notice that his mother was only half as tall as he was. He let Berta push him around in the box until he was lying the way she wanted him to, and he peacefully ate when she thought it was time. He paid no attention at all when she licked him. He was a perfectly content- ed lamb.

Marjory's mother did notice how much Patrick had grown. One day when he was two and a half weeks old she said, "It's April now and getting quite warm. I think Patrick and Berta could move to the side porch. The railing and the gate will keep Patrick from falling off the edge. It's time he had a chance to roam around a bit."

Marjory agreed that Patrick couldn't spend his whole life indoors, but she could- n't help thinking that the kitchen would seem a bit empty without him.

Mr. Miller chose a moment when Berta was out in the yard and Patrick was asleep to move their box. He simply picked it up with Patrick in it, carried it out the door and set it on the porch in a sunny corner.

Patrick didn't seem to mind at all. He lifted his head and looked around but he stayed in the box.

Marjory didn't want Patrick's devoted mother to come into the kitchen and find her baby gone, so she went outside and found Berta having a brief nap beside the lilac bush.

"Come on, Berta," she said. "Patrick has moved to the side porch. I'll show you. You'll both be fine there."

Berta came but she was not pleased. She jumped into the box to sniff Patrick. Then she jumped out again and went to the door. She whined and looked at Marjory.

"No, Berta," said Marjory. "This is where Patrick will live now. That's what Mom says and she's just as stubborn as you are."

Maybe Berta knew she couldn't win or maybe the thought of living with Patrick on the porch didn't really seem so terrible to her. She soon jumped back into the box and settled down by licking Patrick's white spot vigorously. When night came, she didn't bark to come inside. She snuggled up very close to Patrick and went to sleep.

Before bedtime Marjory and her dad went out to look at them in the light that shone through the living-room window. They looked as cozy as ever.

"Berta certainly chose the right baby for a cool night like this," said Mr. Miller. "Now it's Patrick's turn to keep his mother warm."

One week later Marjory came home from school and found Patrick looking over the porch gate while Berta slept. He seemed to be looking longingly at the green spring grass.

"Couldn't Patrick go out in the yard now?" she asked her mother. "I'll watch him. I think he's tired of the porch."

"I agree with you. It's time for him to be outdoors," said Mrs. Miller. "If he had stayed on the farm he'd be out in the pasture with his mother. And if he's in the yard he can start eating grass. You could put him out now and see how he likes it."

Marjory immediately phoned Rosalind and Russell. They had to be on hand for this important moment in Patrick's life.

They came right away. When they arrived, Patrick was still looking over the gate. Berta had woken up and was watching him from the box.

Rosalind opened the gate and Marjory lifted Patrick down the steps. She set him down in a spot where the grass was particularly green.

Before she could move away from Patrick, Berta was standing beside her.

"Amazing," said Russell. "That dog heard the gate open and jumped and instantly she was way over there. I didn't think a dachshund could move so fast."

"Berta, it's okay," said Marjory. But Berta paid no attention to her. She went right up to Patrick, who was standing quietly on the grass looking around. She butted her head against him, trying to push him toward the steps.

"No, Berta," said Marjory. "Leave Patrick alone. He's all right. He can't live in a box forever. It's okay."

She half pulled and half coaxed her reluctant dog over to the steps and sat down beside her. She put her hand on Berta's back to comfort her and felt her whining inside.

"Shhh," she said to her friends. When

she bent close she could hear those very quiet whines and she knew that Berta really did not like what was happening.

Patrick, on the other hand, didn't look at all bothered. He stood on the grass looking around. He seemed quite happy but not inclined to do anything.

"Marjory," said Russell suddenly. "Has Patrick ever said anything? I mean, has he ever made a sound?"

Marjory thought for a minute. "You mean has he ever said *baaaaa*. No. I'm sure he hasn't. That's strange, isn't it?"

"Unusual, anyway. I think lambs usually bleat all the time," said Russell. "I guess it's because he's never heard a sheep make a sound."

"How would Patrick know anything about sheep?" asked Rosalind. "He's lived with the Millers all his life and the only mother he knows is a dog."

They all looked at Patrick, a fine-look-ing lamb, sturdy and grayish-white with a black nose and one fluffy white patch of wool on his shoulder.

"Of course," said Marjory slowly. "Patrick doesn't know he's a sheep." Now they all looked at Berta. "He thinks he's a dog."

"Not only a dog, but a dachshund," said Rosalind. She burst out laughing.

"Well, I'm not sure how much lambs think," said Russell. "But he sure doesn't know much about being a sheep."

Marjory patted Berta. "You've done a good job," she said quietly. "But I think it's our turn to teach Patrick something now."

Berta laid her chin on Marjory's knee and sighed. As for Patrick, he stood happi-ly on the grass and waited to learn how to be a sheep.

Marjory, Rosalind and Russell sat and thought. Berta lay with her chin on Marjory's knee, watching Patrick intently. Patrick began to walk around, exploring this new part of his world.

"How will Patrick learn to be a sheep?" Rosalind wondered.

"What does he really need to know?" asked Russell. "I mean, what do sheep do that Patrick absolutely must learn?"

"Eat grass," said Marjory. "He's supposed to live in our yard and eat grass.

Anyway, he can't go on drinking out of a bottle all his life and he can't eat dog food."

"You're right," said Russell. "A sheep has to eat like a sheep. Whether he sounds like a sheep is not so important."

"I don't suppose he'll start barking," said Rosalind, and she laughed again.

"Or acting like a dog," said Marjory. "Maybe that was the problem with Mary's little lamb. You know, in the song. Maybe he followed her to school because he thought he was a dog." She imagined Patrick trotting along after her to school, refusing to go home. He would follow her right up the stairs and into the classroom.

The song was very realistic, she decided. The children would certainly laugh and Mrs. Kent might laugh a little but then she would say, "You're going to have to take that lamb home, Marjory. He can't stay at school, you know."

How embarrassing. But she would always make sure Patrick was fastened by a long cord to the clothesline post. And he would be eating grass. He wouldn't want to come to school.

"We have to teach him to eat grass," she said firmly. "He can learn everything else about being a sheep on his own."

They all thought some more. How could you teach a lamb to eat grass?

"I refuse to eat grass myself," Russell announced, and both girls nodded. They didn't want to eat grass either.

"Patrick is still almost a baby, isn't he?" Rosalind asked.

"I guess so," said Marjory.

"Well, when my little sister was a baby, we chopped up regular food and just put it in her mouth. It was pretty messy but she learned to chew it up and now she eats everything we do."

"I'll get some scissors," said Marjory.

They used the scissors to chop some nice green grass into very small pieces. Marjory took a pinch in her fingers and stuck it into Patrick's mouth. Patrick looked a bit surprised and sucked hard on her fingers, but he didn't spit out the grass.

"He must have swallowed it," said Russell. "Let me try."

They took turns feeding Patrick pinches of grass. Berta watched from the steps, her eyes following every move.

Finally Rosalind said she had to go home. "I think he's learning something," she said hopefully. Her fingers were a little red and sore from being sucked.

"At least he seems to like the taste of grass," said Russell. "I'm positive he'll want more tomorrow."

Marjory led Patrick back onto the porch. Berta got up from her spot on the

steps and nudged him toward the box.
When he was safely inside and lying down,
she jumped in and sniffed him all over.
Then she went to sleep.

The next day Patrick ate chopped-up
grass from their hands. He nibbled it up
with his lips and chewed and swallowed.
Berta watched closely from the steps.

The day after that they moved on to
what Rosalind called Lesson Three: Eating
Grass from the Ground. Russell put a pile
of chopped-up grass on top of the growing
grass. At first Patrick ignored it, but
Marjory pushed his head down until his
nose was touching the pile. Then he shook
his tail and started to eat. He ate the whole
pile of grass. Then he looked hopefully
around as if he was waiting for more to fall
from the sky.

"He's not brilliant," said Rosalind, "but
I bet he'll catch on tomorrow."

"Are sheep ever brilliant?" said Marjory. "Anyway, he's not a sheep yet. He's just a baby. I think he's doing very well. Right, Berta?" But Berta was sound asleep.

The next day it was Marjory's turn to chop the grass and pile it up for Patrick on the lawn. A smaller pile today. That was Lesson Four in their plan. She wasn't going to give Patrick any help, either. She went and joined the others on the steps, with Berta right beside her as usual.

Patrick made short work of the little heap of grass. He seemed puzzled as he snuffled up the last bits, and he looked at Marjory for a moment. Then he lowered his head and took another bite. This time he was eating the grass that was growing. The children were so quiet that they could hear the grass stems snapping between his teeth.

Patrick lifted his head. Marjory could

see blades of grass sticking out of his mouth. He began to chew. In a moment he had chewed up and swallowed that whole mouthful of grass.

He stood there a moment almost as if he was thinking. Then he opened his mouth and said *baaaaa* quite loudly. He looked a little surprised and then he said it again. *Baaaaaaa*. Then he bent his head and began to eat grass steadily.

Berta lifted her head when Patrick spoke. She didn't move for a moment. Then she sighed a big sigh and stood up.

"It's all right, Berta," said Marjory. "He's just growing up."

But Berta paid no attention. She turned around and crossed the porch toward the house without looking back. She pushed the screen door open with her nose and went inside. They could hear her walk across the living room and up the stairs.

"I guess she thinks Patrick doesn't need her so much now," said Russell. "He's eating grass and he can do that on his own."

"Her job is finished," said Rosalind. "You know Berta isn't the sort to do work that isn't needed."

"I think she knows he's a sheep now. He's not her baby any more," said Marjory. "He told her that when he said *baaaa*. I wonder whether she'll remember that he used to be her baby."

They all sat thinking about that and watching Patrick eat. Just about the time he had finally had enough, Mr. Miller came home.

After Marjory and Rosalind and Russell told him everything that had happened, he said, "You've taught Patrick what he needs to know. He's ready to become a regular farm animal. You and Berta have done a fine job."

"But what will happen to Patrick now?" asked Marjory.

"He'll sleep in the barn. I've got a nice pen all ready for him. And he'll be able to eat grass all day. He will be a very happy sheep."

Marjory knew he was right, but she also knew that she would miss Patrick the lamb. Patrick the sheep wouldn't be quite the same.

When Rosalind and Russell had gone home, she went to find Berta. It wasn't hard since she was back in her old forbidden spot on Marjory's bed. Asleep.

Marjory looked at her sleeping dog. Did she think she had done a fine job? Would she miss Patrick? Would she visit him while he ate grass?"

"Oh, I wish you could talk," she said. She lay down on the bed. Berta moved over a tiny bit to make room for her.

"You're a funny dog," said Marjory. "I don't understand you but it's nice to have you back where you're not supposed to be."

Patrick spent the whole summer eating grass in the Millers' yard. He did such a good job of keeping it trimmed that no one ever had to mow. He grew and grew and his wool was thick. The white patch on his shoulder gradually disappeared, and he was medium gray from head to tail.

He also said *baaaaaa* over and over, all day long.

"Maybe he's waiting for another sheep to answer him," said Russell.

"Or maybe he just likes the sound of his own voice," said Rosalind.

"I love Patrick but I'm tired of the sound of his voice," said Marjory. "I tell him to be quiet, but sheep don't seem to listen very well."

Berta paid no attention to Patrick's voice. In fact, she ignored him completely. She had gone back to her old life of eating, sleeping and short walks.

"Doesn't she miss Patrick at all?" Marjory asked her mother. "She loved him so much."

"She was a very good mother," said Mrs. Miller. "She did the job. But animals don't go on being mothers to their children when their children don't need them any more. And the children forget their mothers. Not like people. We never forget."

It was nice having Berta back at her regular job of wagging her tail when Marjory came home from school and keeping her company while she did her homework. Marjory had to admit that.

"You were a terrific mother," she said to Berta. "But what I like best about you is that you are a dog and a good one, too."

In September Patrick went back to the farm where he would have lots of sheep to talk to. Jack Steiner was very pleased with him and his wool when he came to pick him up.

"I told you he was a good one," he said. "And you folks took real good care of him."

"We had help," said Mr. Miller, looking at Berta. The farmer seemed a little puzzled, but he was in a hurry so he didn't ask questions.

In October Berta had puppies, real dachshund puppies. Mrs. Miller had found a nice dog from a nearby town to be their father, but as far as Berta was concerned, they were her puppies and no one else's.

There were four of them and they were brown just like Berta, but their eyes were closed and their noses were pushed in so that their faces were wrinkly. Their ears were little fat pads that stuck out from the sides of their heads. Mrs. Miller said that they would grow up to look exactly like Berta, but Marjory thought they were darling just the way they were.

Berta became a total mother again. She took charge of the puppies just as she had taken charge of Patrick. And these babies were perfect for her. She could feed them herself. They lined up along her belly sucking away. When they were finished, she could wash them completely, turning them over with her nose and licking them until she decided they were clean. She could curl up around them and keep them cozy in

their box in the kitchen. And everyone, Rosalind included, knew that Berta would protect her babies from any harm.

"Do you think she's so good because she practiced on Patrick?" asked Marjory.

"Practice helps," said her mother. "But I think Berta is just good at being a mother, no matter what sort of babies she has. She knows what to do."

The puppies grew, of course. When their eyes were open and they were beginning to push themselves up on their feet and wobble around their box, Berta sometimes disappeared. The puppies would be squeaking with hunger and Berta nowhere in sight.

Marjory would go upstairs and look under her bed. In the farthest corner she could see a familiar dark shape.

"Berta, come out," she would say sternly. "Your babies are hungry."

Gradually, Berta would creep out and go slowly downstairs to do her job.

"Do you think Berta is bored with her babies?" Marjory asked her father.

"No," he answered. "Every parent needs a break sometimes. And she knows they're big enough to do without her for a while."

Marjory remembered Berta and Patrick curled up together. She remembered how determined Berta was to take over the job of raising Patrick. And she remembered what a big and wonderful baby Patrick turned out to be. She wondered if Berta was just a tiny bit disappointed in her puppies. After all, they would never be sheep.

She mentioned this to Rosalind one day.

"Berta chose Patrick to be her baby," Marjory said. "Maybe she wishes that all her babies would be so special."

"Well," said Rosalind, "don't tell her I said so, but I think that Berta is the one who is special. And I think that any baby of hers will be special, too. In fact, my mother said I could have one of her puppies. Do you think Berta would mind?"

"I'm sure she wouldn't," said Marjory. "In fact, once the puppy grows up and lives at your house, she won't even remember it. Berta likes her babies and then she likes to rest and forget about them. But we'll remember. Imagine, two remarkable dogs right next door to each other. It will be perfect."

Ticket to Curlew
Celia Barker Lottridge

WINNER
Canadian Library Association Book of the Year Award
Geoffrey Bilson Historical Fiction Award

It is 1915, and Sam Ferrier and his father arrive by train in Curlew, Alberta, to build a new home for the family. When they finally reach their parcel of land, Sam can see nothing but endless stretches of grassland and blue sky. It is nothing like their old home in Iowa, and he wonders why his restless father ever decided to bring the family to this lonely, barren land.

In time, though, the house is built, and the rest of the family joins them. Gradually Sam discovers that there is much more to the flat and featureless prairie than he realized. The tall grasses hide a mysterious collection of gleaming white skulls. Torrential thunderstorms appear with startling swiftness out of a clear-blue sky. And when one day he finds that his little brother has suddenly disappeared on the seemingly flat prairie, Sam discovers that their new land can be both awesome and frightening.

ISBN 0-88899-221-1 (paperback)

Wings to Fly
Celia Barker Lottridge

WINNER
IODE National Chapter: Violet Downey Book Award

In *Ticket to Curlew*, Sam Ferrier and his father moved to Canada and built a homestead in the middle of the unsettled prairie. Eventually the rest of the family joined them, and during the first three years they learned to respect their harsh new land and find hidden beauty in its endless grassland.

Eleven-year-old Josie is well settled in her new home now, but she's never had a friend her own age. So when a girl named Margaret moves to the area from England, Josie is glad to have someone with whom she can ride to school, explore the mysterious, abandoned silver house and dream about the future.

But what does the future hold for a young girl in 1918? Could Josie fly airplanes like Katherine Stinson, her heroine?

Will she be a teacher like Miss Barnett? What would it be like to be Margaret's sad mother, who can't bear to unpack her fine English china in the crude sod house that is her new prairie home?

As the year unfolds, Josie searches for more information about the woman aviator. She finds a way to break through Margaret's mother's sadness. And she finally discovers the secret behind the silver house.

ISBN 0-88899-346-3 (paperback)

The Wind Wagon
Celia Barker Lottridge
illustrated by Daniel Clifford

In 1859 the only way to get out west to the Rocky Mountains is by oxcart — and that's a slow journey that takes several months. So when Sam Peppard builds his "wind wagon" — a narrow wooden cart with a large mast in the middle — and announces that he's going to sail across the prairie, everyone scoffs. But Sam sticks to his plan and dreams of mining silver in the Rocky Mountains while waiting for the right wind. And one day, when the wind is almost perfect, he "sets sail" for the West.

Based on a real-life event, this is an exciting and fast-paced story.

ISBN 0-88899-234-3 (paperback)